I0712685

OTTER AND WOLF

A Tale of Friendship, Loss, and Healing

Carolyn Frances Krysiak

Copyright © 2025 by
Carolyn Frances Krysiak

All rights reserved. No part of this book may be
reproduced, distributed, or transmitted in any form
or by any means, including photocopying,
recording, or other electronic or mechanical
methods, without the prior written permission of the
publisher, except in the case of brief quotations
embodied in critical reviews and certain other
non-commercial uses permitted by copyright law.

About the Author

Carolyn F. Krysiak is a therapist and storyteller who writes to help children feel seen, safe, and strong.

Her stories often begin in the playroom, where metaphor becomes a bridge between feeling and understanding. With a heart for healing and an eye for symbolism, she crafts gentle tales that guide young readers through grief, memory, and belonging.

She lives surrounded by music, cats, and creativity—and believes stories can be both a mirror and a lantern for the soul.

Dedication

For the little otters who are brave enough to feel sad, and strong enough to remember. Your wolf is always near.

Acknowledgement

With appreciation for the children who whispered truths in the language of play.

With gratitude to my mother, who celebrated my imagination and cherished my creative nature.

With respect for Leslie Baker, whose mentorship helped me listen more deeply and trust the quiet wisdom of the playroom.

With admiration for my illustrator and creative collaborators—thank you for helping shape this book's soul.

With love for my squirrel—my beloved husband, my companion in wonder—your laughter and steadiness strengthen me.

With humility for the sacred stillness where stories are born—thank you.

May grief find gentleness here, and memory find its voice.

This is the story of
Otter and Wolf
Best of friends

Near a lake
lived an otter.
He loved to play

Every day, his friend
Wolf would come to the
lake to drink and play.

They splashed in the water
until they were tired, and
then they would curl up
together and sleep.

One day, a hunter came to the lake. Otter was alone.

The hunter threw
a net over Otter.
Poor Otter was helpless
he couldn't get out of the net.

As he was struggling,
Wolf arrived.
Wolf was angry.

While they were fighting,
Otter escaped and hid.
Suddenly, Otter heard a
loud bang.

He looked out from his hiding place and saw the hunter limping away.

Wolf was lying on the ground and bleeding. Otter ran to Wolf, but there was nothing he could do. Wolf was dying.

"It's all my fault," said Otter. "If I had been brave, you wouldn't be leaving me."

"No," said Wolf, "it's not. I don't want you to blame yourself. Remember I love you and remember to play."

He missed Wolf.
He no longer felt
like playing.

Some days he was angry. He was mad at himself and remembered everything he ever did wrong. He was mad at the hunter for coming to the lake.

Otter didn't know it, but a squirrel had been watching
him from the treetops all week long.
One day, the squirrel came to the water. He asked why
Otter was sometimes angry and sometimes crying.

At first, Otter didn't want to say. But it
was harder to hold the words back
than it was to speak them.

"My best friend Wolf died recently, and I feel
horrible. I feel like I messed up, and I get angry and
then sad because I cannot change any of it."

When Otter told him this, Squirrel was sad, too. Squirrel's eyes were wet as he listened. They sat together for a little bit, listening to nature, until they both felt calmer.

Then Squirrel told Otter how he was sad when his brother died. He told Otter that he had found a way to still be close to his brother. He showed Otter a special box that he made to keep his brother's favorite acorns in.

Squirrel opened that box and looked at the acorns to remember his brother while he held them in his paws.

Squirrel and Otter thought about Wolf and what might help Otter remember him. Otter said, "I worry that my memories of Wolf will fly away from me and I'll forget more and more of him."

Squirrel suggested that Otter needed a way to catch the good memories and keep them from escaping him.

They decided to make a dream catcher to keep all the positive memories from floating away and hung it in a tree close to Otter's home.

It helped Otter feel better. Whenever he felt sad, he would look up and see the dream catcher and remember the fun he had with Wolf.

Sometimes he talked to Squirrel, too.
They became friends, and Otter began
to play again.

Although Wolf was gone and things
would never be the same, Otter
learned that Wolf would always be
in his heart.

Make a Paper Plate
Dream Catcher

Supply list:

- A paper plate, rigid enough to keep its shape
- Yarn, about 12 feet
- Pony Beads to string on yarn
- Feathers
- Markers or Poster Paint
- Punch to make holes
- Clear Tape

Instructions:

1. Cut out the center of the plate so that you have a large hoop. The hoop should be at least an inch wide.
2. Punch holes around the hoop about 1in apart.
3. Working on the underside of the plate hoop (easier to color) - color or paint as desired.
4. Take 8 feet of yarn and secure one end with sticky tape to the inside of the plate..
5. Weave the yarn through the holes. Add beads as you go, letting them sit on the yarn in the middle of the hoop.
6. Secure the end of the yarn with sticky tape, on the inside of the plate.
7. Punch a hole center top and make a loop to hang up your Dream Catcher.
8. Punch two or three holes along bottom edge for dangles...

   a. For each dangle, take about 1 foot of yarn and secure a bead near the end of the string. Then thread additional beads into the string.
   b. Secure the end of this yarn, above the beads, through the punched hole and secure with sticky tape inside the plate.
   c. Repeat with other one or two dangles.
   d. Tie feathers onto the ends of yarn below the beads.

Made by Carlton family

www.ingramcontent.com/pod-product-compliance
Lightning Source LLC
Chambersburg PA
CBHW041731300726
48981CB00005B/315